Dad,
Aren't You Glad?

written by Lynn Plourde ★ illustrated by Amy Wummer

Dutton Children's Books ★ New York

To Jacob, a great little helper, with love from Aunt Lynn
L.P.

To Mark, world's greatest dad (& husband)
A.W.

Library of Congress Cataloging-in-Publication Data

Plourde, Lynn.
Dad, aren't you glad?/by Lynn Plourde; illustrated by Amy Wummer.—1st ed.
p. cm.
Summary: Although he is too little to take out the garbage, give a piggyback
ride, and perform other tasks as well as his dad can, a young child knows that
there is one thing he can do as well as anyone.
ISBN 0-525-47362-9
[1. Father and child—Fiction. 2. Kissing—Fiction.]
I. Wummer, Amy, ill. II. Title. PZ7.P724Da 2005
[E]—dc22 2004054486

Published in the United States by Dutton Children's Books,
a division of Penguin Young Readers Group
345 Hudson Street, New York, New York 10014
www.penguin.com/youngreaders

Designed by Beth Herzog

Manufactured in China
First Edition

10 9 8 7 6 5 4 3 2 1

Dad, aren't you glad
you have **me** to help you today?

You usually do all the "Dad" stuff,
but now it's **my** turn
so you can rest
on your special day.

Dad, aren't you glad

I'm the one who gets to pour milk

on our cereal today?

And takes out the garbage?

And gives the dog a bath?

And, Dad, aren't you glad

I'm the one who gets to give *you*
a piggyback ride today?

And shuffles the cards for "Go Fish"?

And puts together all the parts to my toys?

Dad, aren't you glad

I'm the one who gets to drive **you** places today?

And pushes the shopping cart?

And pays at the store?

And a great grass cutter?

And can put up the tent so fast?

Well, maybe I still have
some things to learn.

But aren't you glad, Dad,
that there's **one** "Dad" thing
I can do just as good as you?

Smooooooooooch-a-roo!

The Traveling Musicians of Bremen

To Carol,
my children's literature daughter-in-law,
with love

P K P

To Mary Jane

K M D

First U.S. Edition 1992
First published in Canada by Kids Can Press Ltd.

Joy Street Books are published by Little, Brown and
Company (Inc.)

10 9 8 7 6 5 4 3 2 1

Printed in Hong Kong

Library of Congress Cataloging-in-Publication Data

Page, P. K. (Patricia Kathleen), 1916–
     The traveling musicians of Bremen / retold by
P. K. Page ; illustrated by Kady MacDonald
Denton.
          p.   cm.
     Summary: A contemporary adaptation of the
Grimm fairy tale in which four animal friends
mistreated by their masters set out to become
musicians and encounter a den of thieves.
          ISBN 0-316-68836-3
     [1. Fairy tales. 2. Folklore—Germany.] I.
Denton, Kady MacDonald, ill. II. Grimm, Jacob,
1785–1863. Traveling musicians. III. Title.
PZ8.P145Tr   1992
398.2′452′0943—dc20
[E]   91-27094

The Traveling Musicians
of Bremen

Retold by P. K. Page

Illustrated by Kady MacDonald Denton

Little, Brown and Company
Boston Toronto London

I T was one of those beautiful days in summer.
Birds were singing in the leaves.
Wildflowers were blooming in the meadow.
The early morning sun was making diamonds of the dew.
And an old, rather decrepit donkey was munching the sweet grass.
Delicious! Absolutely delicious!
Who wouldn't be happy on such a day?

But the owner of the donkey was not the least bit happy.
He didn't hear the birds.
He didn't even see the sun,
let alone the wildflowers.
Nor could he begin to imagine how good that sweet grass tasted.
All he could see was his donkey.
"Obsolete," he said. "My donkey is obsolete.
Obsolete.
Obsolete.

"Once he carried my grain to market.
Once he pulled my children in a little cart.
Now I have a truck. A big red truck.
And he's obsolete.
Besides which, he's old. And hungry.
All he does is eat."

"Obsolete?" said Donkey, flicking his ears. "That's a word I don't know.
But *old*. He's calling me old. I understand *old*.
I'd better make haste before it's too late."
So with all his might he jumped the gate
and galloped away to the highway.

"I shall go to the city," he said.
"I'll make my name!
I'm a musical chap with a musical soul,
and I'll play the flute for a living."

He had not gone far before he saw a dog lying in the road—
a despondent-looking dog just lying in the road.
"Why, Dog," he said, "you look down in the mouth.
What can be the matter?"

And Dog replied,
"My pedigree is impeccable,
my past performance perfect.
For years I have been a favorite in the house.
And now, just because I am old
and can no longer run when my master goes hunting,
he has threatened to put an end to me.
Why, only this morning he decided to knock me on the head.
Knock me on the head!
I have barely escaped with my life!"

"Cheer up!" said Donkey. "Join company with me.
I'm going to the city to play the flute.
You can play the timpani.
And bark now and then."

And so it came to pass on the highway to the city
that a great, great partnership was formed.
And Donkey and Dog together sang a wonderful, wordless song.

Hee haw Hee haw
Bow wow wow
Hee Bow Haw Wow
Haw Wow How

They had not gone far before they saw a cat,
a ragtaggle cat,
crouched by the side of the highway.

"Oh, Cat," said Donkey, "you've a hangdog look—excusing the expression."
"You would have, too," cried Cat with a wail,
"if you'd just escaped with your ninth life.
Why, only this morning my mistress tried to drown me!
And simply because I am quite off mice.
I no longer like the taste of them at all.
I much prefer to sit before the fire with a saucer full of milk.
Merely to think of it makes me purr."

"Take heart," replied Donkey, "and you shall have *cream*.
We're traveling musicians.
We need a soprano,
and I'll wager you sing like a bird."

Cat felt so much better after this fine compliment that she began to sing.

> *Mee ow Mee ow*
> *Mee ow ow*
> *Mee ow Mee ow*
> *Ow Ow Ow*

"Bravo!" said Donkey.
"What remarkable luck to meet a cat with so dulcible a voice.
Join us, Cat, and you can play the glockenspiel."

So the three of them, now, set off for the city, there to make their names.

They had not gone far before they came across a rooster
crowing from a gate,
crowing with all his might.

Doodle doodle doo
Doodle doodle dee
Doodle dee doodle
Deedle doo dee

"Well done!" said Donkey.

"I do declare that you make the most marvelous din.
But it's long past dawn
to judge by the sun,
so what in the world is the matter?"

"Matter!" said Rooster with an angry flap.
"My mistress plans to give my neck a chop
and put me in a pot
and make me into soup!"

"Nonsense!" said Donkey.
"We can't allow that.
We're off to the city to make names for ourselves.
You've a rousing good voice.
You can carry a tune.
Let us form a quartet."

And so they began to sing.

Hee haw   Hee haw
Bow   wow   wow
Mee ow   Mee ow
Doodle doodle doo
Hee Bow Haw Wow
Mee Doo Arf

Having persuaded Rooster to join them,
they set off once again for the city.

This time, they were in such high spirits
that they danced as they went,
although Donkey was lame
and Dog had an ache
and Cat had a pain
in the tip of her tail
and Rooster, alack,
had a crick in his neck
and his joints were as stiff
as an iron weather vane.
Yet they danced till all four
could not dance one step more.

Besides, darkness was falling,
and, as they were close to a wood,
they decided to settle down for the night.

Donkey and Dog lay under a tree,
Cat on a branch overhead,
while Rooster chose, as was his way,
the topmost branch for bed.

They had only just begun to doze—
the night had hours to go—
when from his lookout in the leaves,
Rooster began to crow.

"Time to get up," barked Dog.
"Surely it's not morning yet!" said Donkey.
"I see a light," said Rooster.
"Well, it can't be the sun," said Donkey. "Look again, friend."
"It might be a house," said Rooster.
"Then let's move," urged Dog.
"I've had better beds than these woods,
and who knows? There might be bones."
"Or milk," said Cat.

So once again they set out,
this time in the direction of the light,
which grew larger and larger
and brighter and brighter,
until they came to a house that was all ablaze with light.

Donkey, being tallest, walked cautiously up to a window
and looked in.
"What do you see?" asked Dog.

"I see a table spread with all kinds of delicious food," said Donkey
in a hoarse whisper.
"And a band of robbers, bold as brass, having
a feast and counting their stolen gold."

"Just the place for us!" barked Dog. "How do we get in?"

So the four musicians came up with a plan.

First Donkey placed his front feet very,
very carefully against the window.

Then Dog jumped onto Donkey's shoulders,
Cat scrambled onto Dog's back,
and finally Rooster flew up and landed
—bop—right on the top of Cat's head.

Then at the arranged
signal, they all
began to sing.

Hee haw Hee haw
Bow wow wow
Mee ow Mee ow

Doodle doodle doo

Hee Bow Haw Wow

Mee Doo Arf

Baw Wee

How wow

Mow Ee Dow

Hee Boo

Boodle Moo

Bee Mee Doo

And at the same moment, they crashed through the glass—
a great furry, feathery, four-headed monster with hooves and claws.

You should have seen those robbers run!

They were sure, for there wasn't a clear conscience among them,
that some terrible hobgoblin was after them.
One and all, they ran lickety-split to the forest.

But in the house, what a feast was spread for the lucky musicians.
Such tidbits and dainties, such mouth-watering bites.
Delicacies beyond anything they had seen on their masters' tables.

They munched and they gobbled and they lapped and they pecked,
and when they had swallowed every bite in sight,
they turned out the light and settled down for the night.

Donkey lay in the yard on a heap of straw.
Dog stretched out behind the door.
Close to the embers of the fire,
Cat curled up like a ball of fur.
And Rooster, high on the topmost beam,
closed his eyes, began to dream.

Soon there was not a sound to be heard.

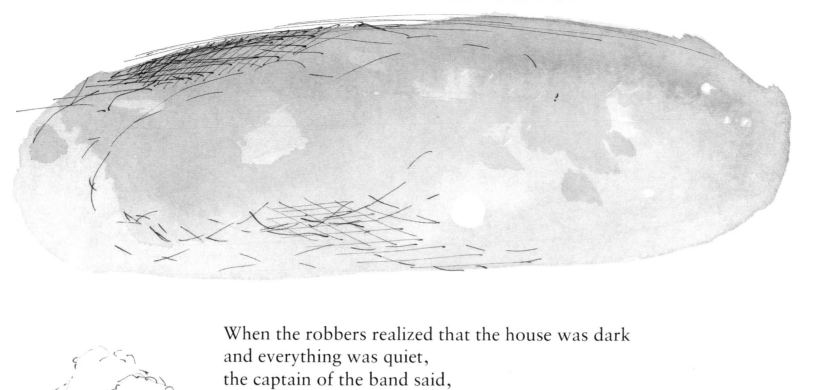

When the robbers realized that the house was dark
and everything was quiet,
the captain of the band said,
"We were fools to be frightened by a mere noise.
Are we cowards, too, to hide all night in the woods?
Robber John, you slip back and find out how things stand."

Shaking a little in his boots as he went,
poor Robber John crept stealthily toward the house.
A twig cracked underfoot and he jumped.
Then . . . total silence.
He couldn't even hear himself breathe.

Reaching the house, he opened the door very carefully.
Apart from the pounding of his heart, he could hear . . . nothing.

Needing a light and mistaking the fiery eyes of Cat for glowing coals,
he blew on them.

Cat spat in his face and dug her claws into his hands.
Dog jumped up and bit him in the leg as he made for the door.
Donkey, wakened from slumber, gave him a well-aimed kick as he passed.
"Cock-a-doodle-doo!" screamed Rooster from his beam overhead.

Poor Robber John, frightened out of his wits,
ran to his friends in the forest,
breathless and nearly fainting.
"There's a terrible witch in the house," he gasped.
"She hissed in my face and scratched me with her long nails.
A murderous villain stabbed me in the leg.
A monster lay in wait in the yard and beat me with a club.
But, worst of all,
on the roof sat the judge, shouting,
'Cock-a-doodle-doo-me, bring the robbers *to* me! *To* me! *To* me!' "

And so the robbers never, but never, returned.

And any day at all, if you happen to pass that house,
whether it be morning, noon, or night,
you will hear the musicians making their music for all who care to listen.

Or for no other reason than the sheer joy of it.